TO EMMA AND ELSIE – M.R.

FOR TOBY AND THE TANGERINE TOWEL – N.L.

Text copyright © 2004 by Michael Rosen
Illustrations copyright © 2004 by Neal Layton

Published by Bloomsbury, New York and London
Distributed to the trade by Holtzbrinck Publishers
Library of Congress Cataloging-in-Publication Data available upon request

ISBN 1-58234-851-0

First U.S. Edition 2003
Printed in China

1 3 5 7 9 10 8 6 4 2

Bloomsbury USA Children's Books, 175 Fifth Avenue, New York, New York 10010

All papers used by Bloomsbury Publishing are natural, recyclable products made
from wood grown in sustainable, well-managed forests. The manufacturing processes
conform to the environmental regulations of the country of origin.

Howler

Michael Rosen   Neal Layton

BLOOMSBURY
CHILDREN'S
BOOKS

Hello. This is me. I write books. I like things to mean just what they're supposed to mean.

Rover is a small human and she is my pet.
Rover is the name that I gave her.
But it doesn't stop there. Oh no.

Rover has a dad
who barks a lot.
I call him Rex.

I call Rover's
mother Cindy.

I have a story to tell today.

It all began when I noticed one day that Cindy was getting bigger.
   She didn't get bigger upwards.
   She started getting bigger outwards.

BIGGER

I thought she had swallowed a big dinner.
But she kept on getting bigger.
  Bigger and bigger and bigger.

The next thing I noticed was that Rex came back
with a new basket for me.

But every time I tried to get in it, they all barked at me.
Loudly.

Then they hung small animals from the ceiling.
I found out they were too high up to chase.

I think I started to understand what was going on when
Cindy gave Rover a book full of very small humans.

Then one day I took Rover to stay with the big human next door. I call her Trixie. Rex and Cindy went off quickly in the family box. Cindy was breathing loudly.

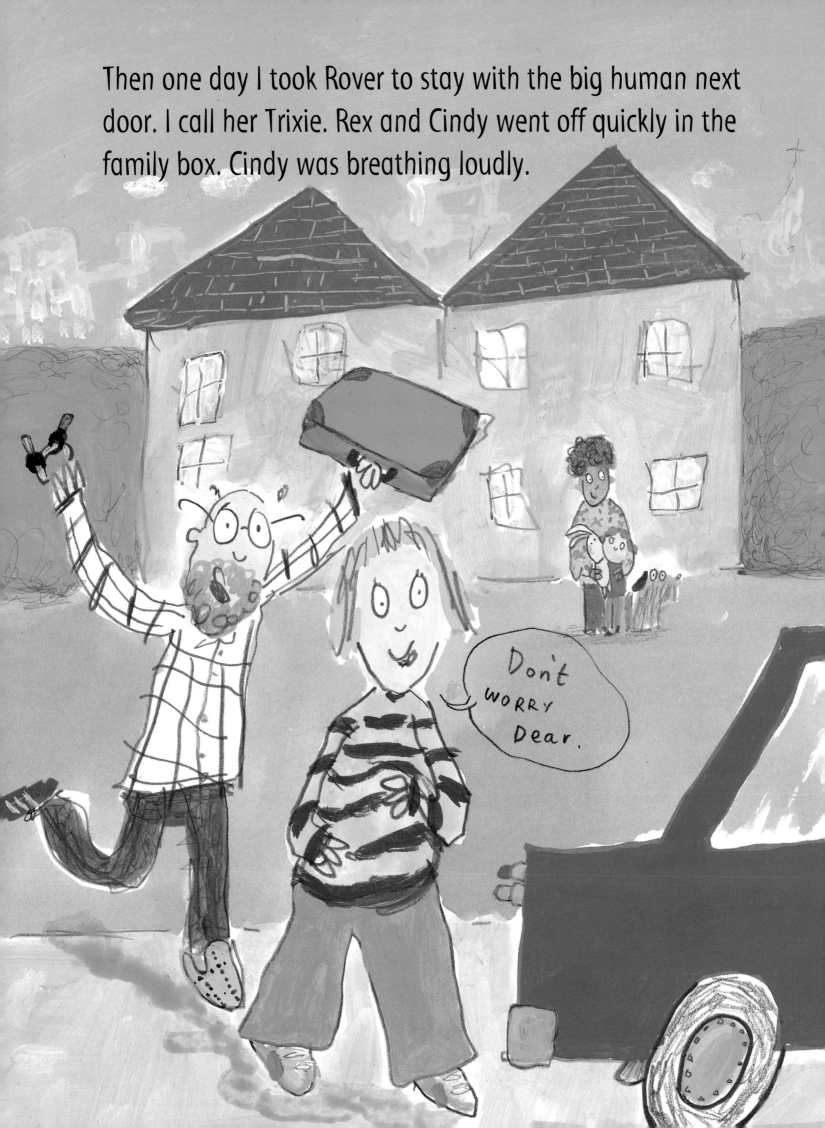

Rover and Trixie pretended to be Rex and Cindy
and squeezed my rabbit.
    Rover looked worried.

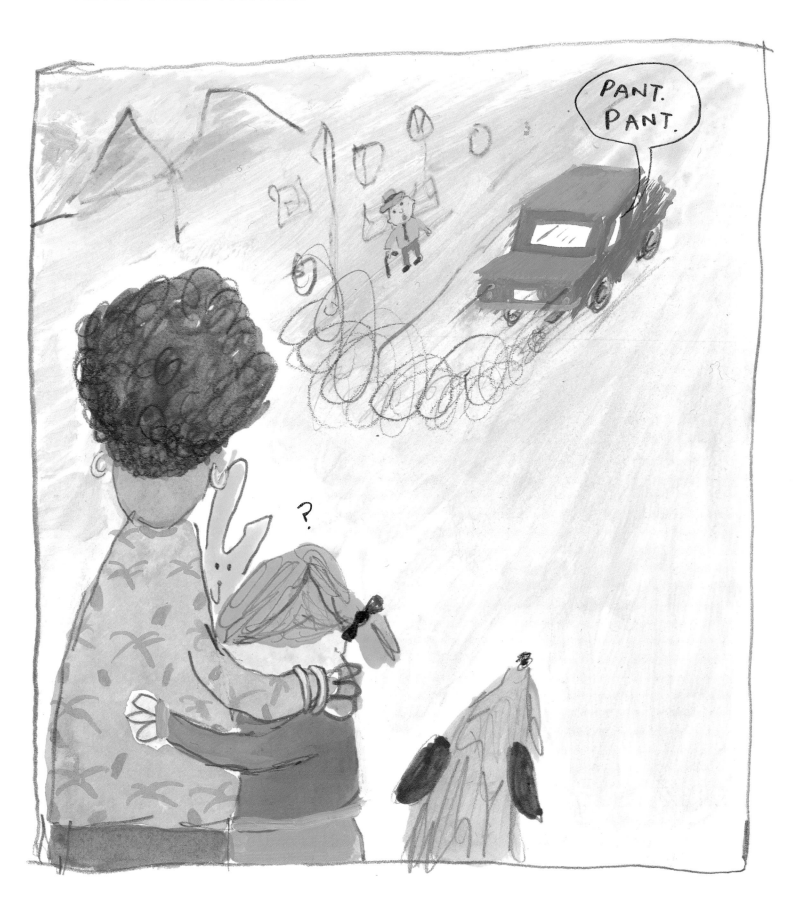

When Rex and Cindy came back they had found a very small human. Rover stared at it. Rover tried to eat it. It tried to eat Cindy.

Most of the time it howled. So I called it Howler. Rex slept.
And no one noticed me.
   No one at all.

I tried wagging my tail.
I went and got the ball in case they had lost it.
I chased my tail very quickly.

But no matter what I did, no one noticed me.

It was time to do something about it. My first plan was to tell Howler to go. Rex woke up and sent me out.

My next plan was to tell Rex and Cindy to go.
Rex woke up again and sent me out.

And then I came up with my great plan. I got friendly with Ruff-ruff. Her pet human is Trixie. So while Rex and Cindy and Rover were busy with Howler, I spent some time with my friend, Ruff-ruff.

Not long after Ruff-ruff got bigger. Not longwards. Outwards. And then one day she had five small ones. Ruff-ruff called them Rufflets. I thought they all ought to be called Small Me, but I wasn't asked.

Rover came and looked at the Rufflets and barked.
Rex woke up. He came and looked and barked.
Cindy came to look. She barked. Trixie came to look.
She barked.

Everyone came to look. Except for Howler.

Then I made up my mind. I think that as long as Rex and Cindy and Rover and Trixie say it's OK for the Rufflets to stay, then it's OK for Howler to stay.

I won't tell Howler to go. But maybe that's because I know who Rover likes best.

US